The Tiara Club

Club

at Silver Towers

For Judith Elliott,
with love and admiration
xx VF

For Rosa, thanks for

www.tiaraclub.co.uk

ORCHARD BOOKS
338 Euston Road, London NW1 3BH
Orchard Books Australia
Hachette Children's Books
Level 17/207 Kent St, Sydney NSW 2000

A Paperback Original

First published in Great Britain in 2006
Text © Vivian French 2006
Illustrations © Sarah Gibb 2006

The rights of Vivian French and Sarah Gibb to be
identified as the author and illustrator of this work
have been asserted by them in accordance with
the Copyright, Designs and Patents Act, 1988.

A CIP catalogue record for this book is available
from the British Library.

ISBN 978 1 84616 196 4

7 9 10 8 6

Printed in China
Orchard Books is a division of Hachette Children's Books,
an Hachette UK company.
www.hachette.co.uk

The Tiara Club
at Silver Towers

Princess Katie
and the Dancing Broom

By Vivian French
Illustrated by Sarah Gibb

ORCHARD BOOKS

The Royal Palace Academy
for the Preparation of Perfect Princesses

(Known to our students as *"The Princess Academy"*)

OUR SCHOOL MOTTO:
*A Perfect Princess always thinks of others
before herself, and is kind, caring and truthful.*

Silver Towers offers a complete education for Tiara Club princesses with emphasis on selected outings. The curriculum includes:

Fans and Curtseys	*Problem Prime Ministers*
A visit to Witch Windlespin	*A visit to the Museum of Royal Life*
(Royal herbalist, healer and maker of magic potions)	*(Students will be well protected from the Poisoned Apple)*

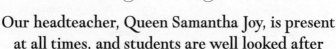

Our headteacher, Queen Samantha Joy, is present at all times, and students are well looked after by the school Fairy Godmother, Fairy Angora.

Our resident staff and visiting experts include:

LADY ALBINA MacSPLINTER (School Secretary)	*QUEEN MOTHER MATILDA (Etiquette, Posture and Poise)*
CROWN PRINCE DANDINO (School Excursions)	*FAIRY G (Head Fairy Godmother)*

We award tiara points to encourage our Tiara Club princesses towards the next level. All princesses who win enough points at Silver Towers will attend the Silver Ball, where they will be presented with their Silver Sashes.

Silver Sash Tiara Club princesses are invited to return to Ruby Mansions, our exclusive residence for Perfect Princesses, where they may continue their education at a higher level.

PLEASE NOTE:
Princesses are expected to arrive at the Academy with a *minimum* of:

Twenty ball gowns
(with all necessary hoops, petticoats, etc)

Twelve day dresses

Seven gowns
suitable for garden parties, and other special day occasions

Twelve tiaras

Dancing shoes
five pairs

Velvet slippers
three pairs

Riding boots
two pairs

Cloaks, muffs, stoles, gloves and other essential accessories as required

Hello, and how are you?
Thank you SO much for being at
Silver Towers with us... Oh! You do know
who we are, don't you? I'm Princess
Katie, and I share the Silver Rose Room
with the Princesses Charlotte, Alice,
Emily, Daisy and Sophia. We're all
trying really hard to win our
Silver Sashes – but it's hard work
getting Tiara Points, especially
when those HORRIBLE
twins are around...

Chapter One

"Gruella darling, could you ask Daisy to pass the marmalade? Nobody here has ANY manners, even though they're supposed to be princesses!"

We were sitting having our breakfast, and as usual the twins were showing off. Princess Diamonde was so near the marmalade she could easily have reached it herself.

I looked at Daisy, and she was staring at her plate. She didn't seem to have heard Diamonde at all. Alice leant across the table and thumped the jar down, right under Diamonde's nose.

"Your marmalade, Your Majesty," she said.

"Sorry to have troubled you, I'm sure," Diamonde said in a sneery voice, and tipped at least half the jar onto her toast.

Sophia was sitting next to Daisy, and she'd noticed how quiet she was too.

"Are you all right?" she asked.

Daisy shook her head.

At once we all clustered round her, asking what was wrong. Daisy is so lovely, and she's SO kind...none of us wanted her to be unhappy.

"It's the school outing," Daisy said, and she sounded very wobbly. "I don't want to go. I'm scared!"

"What outing?" I asked. I hadn't heard about any outings – but I'm not always very good at remembering to read what's on our noticeboard. I certainly hadn't that morning – I'd only just been in time for breakfast.

Emily and I had seen a row of coaches crossing the courtyard with the most gorgeous horses, so we'd just HAD to sneak out and watch...and then the bell had rung and we'd zoomed back in.

"Oh dear," said a loud voice behind me. "You mean you haven't heard that we're going to meet a WITCH?" Gruella sniggered. "Maybe you could ask for a spell to make Daisy braver!" And she flounced away, cackling at her own joke just as if she was a witch herself.

I ignored her, and grabbed Charlotte. "Are we really going to meet a witch?"

Charlotte nodded, her eyes shining. "It was on the board this morning! Fairy Angora's taking us! We're going to spend the afternoon with Witch Windlespin, and hear about Good Magic—"

Exactly at that moment, Crown Prince Dandino bounced into the breakfast hall, followed by Lady Albina, the school secretary. Prince Dandino's in charge of arranging outings and excursions, and he was looking SO excited, but Lady Albina was looking really gloomy.

Alice chuckled in my ear. "My big sis told me Lady Albina hates trips out!" she whispered. "She thinks we'll all get lost!"

"Now, my dear young princesses," Prince Dandino said, "We have such a VERY special treat for you today. As you may know, Queen Samantha Joy thinks it is a Very Good Thing for you to see how other people live their lives—" he stopped for a second to give Lady Albina SUCH a superior look – "and Witch Windlespin has very kindly offered to show you her beautiful home. The coaches will be leaving immediately after lunch, so please be ready! Fairy Angora will meet you at the main door at two o'clock precisely – don't be late!" And he bounced away.

Lady Albina sniffed disapprovingly. "If you look at the board you will find out which coach you are travelling in," she snapped. "And please make sure you wear your name badges, and do EXACTLY as you're told!"

As Lady Albina stalked out of the breakfast hall, I gave Daisy a hug, and Emily, Charlotte, Alice and Sophia did too.

"You'll be fine!" I told her. "What could happen when you've got US to look after you?"

And Daisy looked SO much happier as we went off to our morning lessons.

Chapter Two

We hadn't been on any outings before – well, only on very special occasions, like the time we flew on a dragon to King Percival's party. It felt quite strange to be trundling away from Silver Towers that afternoon.

There was another coach in front of us, and two more behind.

Luckily, we'd managed to avoid Gruella and Diamonde. They were in the last coach, which they weren't very happy about at all!

"Where do you think Witch Windlespin lives?" I asked the others.

"I don't know,' Charlotte said. "I hope it's not a dark creepy cave full of spiders!"

"I know!" Alice interrupted. "She lives in the middle of Hollyberry Wood, and she's famous for her magic cures. She does spinning and weaving as well, and her house is full of wonderful cushions and rugs and stuff. She makes her own clothes, too, in the most fabulous colours!"

"She makes clothes?" Emily sounded amazed. "That doesn't sound very witchy!"

"I thought witches always wore black," Katie said. "With pointy hats."

Daisy nodded. "Me too. And they have warts on their noses, and whiskers on their chins. And they put horrid spells on princesses!"

"Queen Samantha Joy would never let us go near anyone like that," Sophia pointed out. "Didn't you ever read the prospectus? It says we're 'well looked after at

all times'. It wouldn't look very good for Silver Towers if we fell into an enchanted sleep for a hundred years!"

That made us laugh, even Daisy, and as the coach began bumping and rattling up a pretty leafy lane I decided I was really looking forward to meeting Witch Windlespin.

We finally stopped outside the sweetest little house nestling under a big oak tree. Fairy Angora was waiting by the tiny front door, and we tumbled out of the coach as fast as we could.

"Be sure to mind your heads as you go in," she warned us. "Listen very carefully, and don't be surprised by anything you see!" And she pushed the door open, and we tiptoed inside.

It was extraordinary! The door was so small, but the moment we were inside we found ourselves in an enormous room, with a wonderful ceiling painted with sparkly stars, and fat rosy babies holding trumpets and puffing out their cheeks. And then I saw there were little ships sailing in between the stars, and they were really moving, and the babies were playing at blowing them this way and that – it looked such fun!

I was so busy staring up at the ceiling that I jumped when something touched my arm.

"Oh! Excuse me!" I said – and

found I was talking to a broom!
And it actually bowed to me!
I was so astonished I couldn't say
anything at all.

"I see my broom has taken a fancy to you, dear Princess Katie!" said a wonderfully deep voice, and I saw Witch Windlespin smiling at me.

She was tall, and although she wasn't exactly beautiful she had the kindest, wisest face…and I suddenly knew she was very very VERY old.

She was dressed in a glorious shimmering golden silk gown with a fringed emerald green shawl round her shoulders, and there were golden lilies shining in her hair.

"Welcome to you, and all your friends," she said. "This is my home. Please come and sit down!"

The cottage was one of the most gorgeous places I've ever been.

There was a roaring fire, and in front of the fireplace were heaps and heaps of the softest rainbow coloured cushions, and floaty wool rugs and blankets. The students from the first coach were already sitting there looking so cosy...and a little black kitten was curled up on Princess Lisa's knees! The six of us found our way to a heap of plumped up indigo and purple pillows, and sank into them as if we were settling into a heap of clouds. I don't think I've ever been so comfortable. I lay back, and watched the babies blowing the ships...and it was absolutely heavenly. I could feel my eyelids drooping, when suddenly there was an incredibly loud KNOCK! KNOCK! KNOCK! on the door.

Witch Windlespin had been arranging some pots and bottles on a table, and she looked up in surprise. "Goodness! I thought Fairy Angora was still outside... Princess Katie, would you let them in?"

Of course I jumped up and hurried to the door. At once Gruella and Diamonde came barging past me, pushing the door open wide.

Chapter Three

The twins paused once they were inside, and stared rudely round.

"Well!" Diamonde said in her poshest voice. "So THIS is a witch's house! Just fancy!"

Gruella tossed her head. "I just don't know what Mummy would say if she saw us here!"

Instead of being cross, Witch

Windlespin gave the horrible twins a beautiful smile. "I knew your great grandmother, my dears – Queen Ethelberta. She was a very particular friend of mine, and I'm so pleased to meet you. Do sit down."

Gruella and Diamonde didn't know WHAT to do. They made a noise like a balloon losing its air, and sat down with a flump. I caught Alice's eye, and I knew she was trying not to laugh.

*

The rest of our year followed the twins in through the door, and then Fairy Angora appeared, looking hot and bothered.

"I'm so sorry," she said. "I left Lady Albina's lists in the coach, and I had to run and fetch them. She'd be so angry if I forgot them!"

Witch Windlespin waved Fairy Angora to a comfortable armchair. As she sat down to mark the register the little black kitten jumped on her lap, and started purring loudly.

"Just rest, darling Angora," Witch Windlespin said. "I'm going to show the princesses how I make a delicious potion for soothing away anxiety and fear. Now, who shall I have to help me..."

She seemed to be looking at Daisy, and I knew Daisy would be really nervous if she was chosen, so I quickly put up my hand.

"Thank you, Princess Katie. Please come and join me."

I did feel a little bit anxious as I walked over to the table covered in strangely shaped jars and bottles, but I needn't have worried. It was so easy! I read out the names of the different herbs, and Witch Windlespin stirred them into a big silver bowl. It wasn't long before a gorgeous smell began to fill the air.

"One final ingredient," said

Witch Windlespin at last.

I read, "Essence of purest pine!" and Witch Windlespin poured a beaker of golden liquid into the bowl with a flourish. At once a burst of tiny stars flew out with a FIZZZZZ.

"There!" Witch Windlespin poured the potion into a crystal bottle, and held it up so we could see how wonderfully clear and sparkly it was. "Perfect! And now, just for fun, why don't some of you try, so you can see just how simple these potions are? Katie, let's see what you can do. Charlotte and Sophia can try as well, with Diamonde, Emily, Daisy and Alice. Oh, and Gruella."

My friends got up and came to join me by Witch Windlespin's table. For a wonderful moment I thought Diamonde and Gruella weren't going to come – but the broom whisked behind them, and gently pushed them forward.

"Fancy us making a potion, Gruella!" Diamonde said in her loudest voice.

"It looks exactly the same as cooking to me," Gruella simpered, "and Mummy always asks us to tell the cooks what

to do, doesn't she, Diamonde?"

I thought Witch Windlespin
might tell them off for being so
boastful, but she didn't say
anything. She fetched a clean
bowl, and put it down among the
herbs and oils.

"Take your time," she said quietly, "and try to think peaceful thoughts as you mix and blend the herbs. Remember your innermost wishes may well be revealed in the potion you make, so do be careful!"

She smiled, and drifted away to show the other princesses her dried flowers, and the plants she used for dyeing her wools.

Chapter Four

It had looked so easy when Witch Windlespin did it – but it was really difficult when we tried. All the herbs got muddled up, and Gruella and Diamonde grabbed for the same bottle of oil and it spilt everywhere.

Diamonde tried to stir the mixture too fast, and it slopped

over the edge, and the most
PECULIAR smell drifted up into
the air. Gruella knocked a basket
of lavender onto the floor, and
I was certain we were going to
end up with a horrible mess.

"Do you think we should tell
Witch Windlespin we can't do it?"
I asked.

To my surprise, Daisy shook her
head. "Why don't we try again?"
she suggested.

Alice said, "Yes!" and so did
Sophia.

Emily, Daisy and Charlotte
nodded.

Diamonde and Gruella folded

their arms and glared. "WE don't want to start again," Gruella said.

The broom suddenly hopped forward, and swept up the lavender. Then it skipped onto the table, and in no time at all the herbs were in neat piles, and the oil stains were gone.

"Thank you!" I said, surprised.
"Oh, thank you so much!"
The broom bobbed a little bow,
and leant itself against the wall.

"DO let's try again," Alice said. "I'm sure we could get it right if we try!"

The broom seemed to nod encouragingly, and we all laughed. Diamonde and Gruella pretended they hadn't seen it.

"Come on, then," I said, so Alice and Charlotte mixed up the herbs, Emily and Sophia poured in the oils, and Daisy and I stirred it. When it was Daisy's turn she stirred it very carefully with her eyes shut tight.

"I'm trying to think peaceful thoughts," she explained.

I was glad she was, because

49

I was BOILING inside. Gruella and Diamonde hadn't offered to help even once. I looked at them as I stirred, and I so nearly said something horrid that I actually had to bite my tongue. Inside my head I was wishing and wishing they weren't there. If only they'd go away, I thought, the rest of us would have such a fabulous time. But I didn't say anything. Then, the absolute minute we'd finished, THEY were the ones who put their hands up.

"Witch Windlespin!" Gruella called out, and she sounded SO angelic, "we've finished! We've made the potion!"

"That's right," Diamonde said, and she gave me a FREEZING stare. "And we did every bit of it all by ourselves!"

If Witch Windlespin noticed me glaring at the twins she didn't say anything. She picked up the bowl, and held it to her nose with her eyes half shut.

"H'mmmmmmm," she said thoughtfully. As she put the potion down, the little black

kitten jumped off Fairy Angora's lap and came running to see what we were doing. It brushed against my leg and made me jump, and I knocked the table – and the bowl wobbled madly. Half the contents splashed over the broom – and it VANISHED!

Everybody gasped – except me.

I knew whose fault it was the broom had disappeared.

Mine.

I'd been wishing so hard that Gruella and Diamonde would go away that my thoughts had got muddled up in our potion...and I'd made a BAD magic.

Chapter Five

I didn't know WHAT to do. Even Witch Windlespin was looking shocked.

"Goodness," she said. "I didn't expect that to happen! And my best broom, too!" She turned to Gruella and Diamonde. "May I ask what you were thinking when you made this?"

If I hadn't been feeling so utterly and completely dreadful, I'd have laughed. Gruella went yellow, and Diamonde went red, and they both opened and shut their mouths like goldfish.

Witch Windlespin looked at the potion, and frowned.

"It's beautifully made," she said, "but there's something very wrong with it."

A sudden wild idea hit me. If I went after the broom, maybe I could bring it back!

"Please," I said, "please – this is all my fault—" and I shut my eyes tight and plunged my hand into the bowl.

I waited to disappear — but nothing happened.

I just started sneezing and sneezing and SNEEZING and I didn't think I'd ever be able to stop. And then Gruella and Diamonde started sneezing too, so hard that everything flew off the table except the bowl of magic potion. Herbs scattered everywhere, bottles crashed to the floor – oh, you've never seen such a mess!

Fairy Angora came hurrying

out of her chair, but Witch
Windlespin held up her hand.

"Let them sneeze their wishes
away!" she commanded, and
the three of us sneezed and
sneezed and sneezed...until
gradually I stopped, and then
Gruella stopped, and finally
Diamonde stopped too.

"I really am very VERY sorry," I whispered. "Will your broom ever come back?"

"See for yourself," said Witch Windlespin, and she pointed at the wall.

At first I couldn't see anything, but all of a sudden I saw bristles...and then the handle... and there was the broom!

"Oh!" I was so pleased to see it again I curtsied to it. "I'm so very sorry I made you disappear!"

The broom gave a little hop and a skip.

"There," Witch Windlespin said. "No harm done."

"But what happened?" Fairy Angora asked. Witch Windlespin looked straight at me, and I knew what I had to do. I curtsied to the two grown-ups. Then I took a deep breath and curtsied to Gruella and Diamonde as well.

"I'm TRULY sorry," I said. "I was wishing that Gruella and Diamonde weren't here." I swallowed hard. "I know I'm very lucky to have my five special friends, and I do know I should be happy when other princesses join in with us, but...but I failed."

"Thank you, Katie," said Witch Windlespin. "And now, Gruella and Diamonde – what have you to say?"

I was sure the twins would say it wasn't their fault, but I was wrong.

Gruella gave a sort of gulp, and said, "I'm sorry too."

"Gruella!" Diamonde was horrified.

But Gruella went on. "I was wishing KATIE wasn't here. You were too, Diamonde – you know you were! She's so good at everything and she was so kind to Daisy, and—" two huge tears rolled down Gruella's cheeks, "it makes everyone love her and nobody ever loves me!"

And she began to cry.

Can you guess what I did next?

I hugged Gruella. Does that sound odd? But she looked SO miserable, I couldn't help it.

Then Diamonde said, "I suppose I'm sorry too." It didn't sound much as if she meant it, but Witch Windlespin smiled, as if she believed every word.

"Good," she said. "And now let's look at the potion!"

We crowded round the table to look, and it was as clear and sparkling as the mixture Witch Windlespin had made!

"Excellent!" she said. "Don't you think, Fairy Angora, that these princesses have done well?"

Fairy Angora looked at us proudly. "Yes!" she said. "Ten tiara points each!"

"But we don't deserve them!" Gruella burst out.

"Gruella dear, you've learnt something MUCH more important than how to make a potion," Witch Windlespin told her.

Gruella looked so happy she positively GLOWED! Diamonde was staring glumly at the floor, but she gave a little nod.

"Right!" Witch Windlespin sounded brisk. "Now, let's have some fun! Katie, would you ask the broom to tidy us up?"

Chapter Six

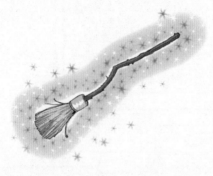

I turned to look at the broom,
and it gave a couple of twirls and
bowed a deep bow to me.
I curtsied back.

"Please, dear broom," I said,
"would you make us tidy?"

At once the broom went mad!
It whizzed about piling the
cushions on one side of the room,

and it whisked away the table, and tidied the pots and bottles onto a shelf – and the room was spotlessly clean and empty!

Witch Windlespin clapped her hands, and oh! It was so AMAZING! The rosy-cheeked cherubs on the ceiling put their trumpets to their lips and began to play – and it was such catchy music we couldn't help but start dancing. Even the kitten began prancing about! I did a little waltz with the broom, and I was about to grab Alice when a thought struck me.

I curtsied my very best curtsey to

Gruella. "Would your Royal Highness do me the honour of dancing with me?"

Gruella curtsied back. "It would

be my pleasure," she said – and off we went, round and round and ROUND the room until we were dizzy and had to stop...

...and at exactly that moment the front door flew open, and a shower of twinkly stars drifted down from the ceiling. In came Prince Dandino beaming from ear to ear, and behind him came a trail of little pageboys carrying boxes and boxes of the most

DELICIOUS Royal Pizza. We scurried to sit among the rainbow cushions for a pizza party...it was such fun! We all chatted and laughed, and the cherubs played softer sweeter music, and it was MAGIC.

*

As the carriages rolled away from Witch Windlespin's house late that afternoon I gave a huge happy sigh.

"Wasn't it a LOVELY day?" I said.

"It was gorgeous," Daisy agreed, and then she grinned at me. "And I wasn't frightened... not once."

"It must have been Witch Windlespin's potion for soothing away anxiety and fear," Charlotte said sleepily.

"No it wasn't," Daisy told her. "It was having all of you to look after me. Especially Katie!"

"We look after each other," I said, and it was true. My friends were just the very best ever, and I was SO lucky to be at Silver Towers...and I'm so very VERY glad you're here with us as well.

What happens next?
Find out in

Princess Daisy
and the Magical Merry-Go-Round

Hello! I'm Daisy. Princess Daisy.
And I do hope you're enjoying being
at Silver Towers with us. You're exactly
the right kind of princess, you
know - just like my lovely friends,
Charlotte, Katie, Alice, Sophia and Emily.
And not at all like Diamonde and
Gruella - they're SO big-headed.
Do you get nervous before you do
something new? I do - I try SO hard
not to, but I can't help it. And learning
to be a Perfect Princess means
we're ALWAYS doing new things,
or going to new places...

Check out

The Tiara Club

website at:

www.tiaraclub.co.uk

You'll find Perfect Princess games and fun
things to do, as well as news on the Tiara
Club and all your favourite princesses!

Win a Tiara Club
Perfect Princess Prize!

Look for the secret word in mirror writing hidden in
a tiara in each of the Tiara Club books. Each book
has one word. Put together the six words from books
7 to 12 to make a special Perfect Princess sentence,
then send it to us together with 20 words or more on
why you like the Tiara Club books. Each month, we
will put the correct entries in a draw and one lucky
reader will receive a magical Perfect Princess prize!

Send your Perfect Princess sentence, your name
and your address on a postcard to:
THE TIARA CLUB COMPETITION,
Orchard Books, 338 Euston Road,
London, NW1 3BH

Australian readers should write to:
Hachette Children's Books,
Level 17/207 Kent Street, Sydney, NSW 2000.

Only one entry per child.
Final draw: 31 August 2007

By Vivian French
Illustrated by Sarah Gibb

The Tiara Club at Silver Towers

All priced at £3.99.

The Tiara Club books are available from all good bookshops, or can be ordered direct
from the publisher: Orchard Books, PO BOX 29, Douglas IM99 1BQ.
Credit card orders please telephone 01624 836000 or fax 01624 837033 or visit our
Internet site: www.wattspub.co.uk or e-mail: bookshop@enterprise.net for details.

To order please quote title, author, ISBN and your full name and address.
Cheques and postal orders should be made payable to "Bookpost plc.©
Postage and packing is FREE within the UK
(overseas customers should add £2.00 per book).

Prices and availability are subject to change.